THE
DERELICT

The Derelict

Neil Williams

BLACK
SHUCK
BOOKS

Black Shuck Books
www.blackshuckbooks.co.uk

First published in Great Britain in 2014 by Pendragon Press
This edition first published in 2021 by Black Shuck Books

All content © Neil Williams 2021
Cover design and interior layout © WHITEspace, 2021
www.white-space.uk

978-1-913038-63-2

For Michelle and Tallis

You may well take me for some old mad drunkard. And why wouldn't you? You've seen how I stagger about this alehouse. How they all avoid my eye. But here, sit beside me and don't let the sight of this crippled hand trouble you. For the price of a drink I'll tell how I got this scar on my forehead. Or how about this tattoo? Isn't she magnificent? I move my arm like so and look, it's like she's dancing for you. Almost like the real thing. Hah! Better you might say; she won't slap your face.

The sun is low to the west. I look out across an ocean that shimmers like quicksilver.

Here, buy me a drink and I'll tell you of my encounter with pirates off the coast of Sarawak, or about the time pack-ice crushed the ship beneath us – I didn't board a ship expecting a two hundred mile walk across a frozen wilderness. But I am not mad and I am not drunk – not yet anyhow. Years spent on a pitching, rolling deck, battered by freezing waves, have robbed me of my balance. Even here on this unyielding, dead rock I still feel the swell of the ocean.

I see a dark shape on the horizon.

In my dreams it's like I never left the sea. Or maybe it never left me. You can't imagine it until you've seen it with your own eyes. In all directions water stretches out as far as the eye can see. And the sky above matches it all the way.

It's a ship I see. But with her sails still furled how can she possibly keep pace with us?

No, I can see in your eye what it is you want to know. Why does an old salt like myself, after years spent sailing the world's oceans, want to spend his final years in this, our most land-locked county? Well go ahead, ask away. I won't bite. But buy me a drink first, and one for yourself. I think you might need it.

There are two pale hands, one hand slowly being placed over the other, climbing up the swaying rope from out of the darkness.

~

"It's a brig right enough. But with no sails hoisted I can't really see it being the same one you saw yesterday," said the skipper as he lowered the telescope and rubbed at his heavily-bearded chin with the eyepiece. After a moment lost in thought he offered me the glass.

I raised the telescope to my good eye and located the bobbing vessel. She was a twin-masted brigantine. From prow to stern she was some eighty to ninety feet in length, with a beam of perhaps a little under twenty. Even on a day as calm as this I struggled to keep the telescope centred on the ship. The rolling North Sea carried both vessels from trough to peak and then down again. I found my view frequently interrupted by foam-flecked walls of green water.

"I see no sign of her crew," I said, scanning the deck. "The dinghy's still lashed amidships and…" I trailed off as I saw the two bare masts. A few tattered ropes flailed as the ship pitched into the next trough. "There are no sails, no sails at all. They appear to have been torn from both yard and boom."

"Caught in a storm most likely," said the captain. I nodded in agreement and handed the telescope back to him.

"I s'pose we'll be taking a closer look, eh skipper?" asked Briggs, the mate, who'd been silently watching us from the helm.

The captain turned to us both.

"In the circumstances, we have no other choice," he nodded to me. "See to it Mister Gilling."

With that, he turned on his heel and went below decks.

~

Up until that point our voyage had been unremarkable. We'd departed the city of Wismar fully laden with a cargo of asphalt, bound for the port of Hartlepool. A brisk north-easterly filled our sails as we crossed the shimmering Baltic. We set a course for Kiel, intent on reaching the open North

Sea by way of the Eider canal. This route meant we avoided the long detour around the Jutland peninsular.

Our ship was a fine German built triple-masted schooner called the *Albin Grau*. All heads counted we were a crew of eight. The skipper had the appearance of as grizzled an old sea-dog as you could wish to meet, so I was surprised to learn he'd spent almost all his early life in landlocked Wiltshire. I was never to discover what had driven him from the relatively sedate life of a landlubber. I'd grown up on the Norfolk coast and the ocean was in my blood. You might even say it was my calling, and I pursued a career at sea with an almost religious fervour; I wonder now if it perhaps fulfilled the same need in me as God did in those more pious than myself. By fourteen I was a cabin boy on an East India Clipper.

I'd joined the *Albin Grau* as second mate at the invitation of Briggs, the first mate. We'd served together many years previously. The steward, and also our cook, was a grim faced Russian called Dmitry. No-one ever spoke his surname and I never took the trouble to enquire of it, so he remained just Dmitry to us all. He was without a doubt the most superstitious of the crew; quite possibly of anyone I'd ever shipped with – and sailors are a superstitious lot at the best of times.

Perhaps more so in the better times, as it was then that things usually took a turn for the worse. He had a small whale-bone pipe that permanently hung from his lower lip. I don't think I ever saw him remove it. Or even smoke from it for that matter.

Of the other sailors, one, Gorski, was Polish and the remaining three, Nemetz and the two Schröders, were German. They were a competent, enthusiastic lot who, with one exception, spoke little English. My smattering of German saw me called upon as interpreter on the numerous occasions when Nemetz was otherwise engaged. Dmitry had little time for any of them. *"Ballast!"* he would bark if any one of them strayed into his path.

It was as we left the inland waterways of Schleswig-Holstein and entered the North Sea that I noticed a ship on the horizon. There was nothing special or indeed unusual in that, as these were busy shipping lanes. But I had started to notice over the duration of that first day in open water that the ship, whose square set mainmast revealed her to be a brigantine, was keeping a steady pace with us. I considered this strange as I could detect no sign of an unfurled sail on either mast. I occasionally lost sight of the vessel and, with my attention directed to other tasks, I would find her slipping from my mind – only for the ship to reappear again during some quiet moment when I let my gaze return to that vast churning emptiness.

Over the course of that day it had become a cause of distraction. It tugged at the periphery of my vision like a mote of dust I seemed unable to rub away. I soon started to wonder if it was truly there or if it was some defect within the eye itself.

That night I took first watch. I kept a careful eye on the horizon where, in the fading light, I'd last seen the ship. It proved to be a particularly dark night. A heavy pall of cloud covered the moon and beyond the ineffectual radiance of the schooner's lanterns I could see nothing. How much more desolate the ocean seems when you can't even see the horizon. I imagined that we might as well be traversing the eternal and indifferent emptiness of the heavens, a votive candle adrift on a sea of India ink. The darkness seemed to grow into an almost tangible barrier around our ship. But still I stared out, hoping to catch any tell-tale sign that the other vessel was still out there. I'm sure that even the orange glow of burning tobacco would have shone out like a beacon in that absolute black.

I was not the only one on deck at that time. From my position at the wheel I had a good view down to the fo'c'sle where I could see Dmitry, pipe in mouth, refuelling the lanterns. On the deck below,

Schröder senior leant against the wooden rail that circled the mizzen-mast. He was whittling at some piece of driftwood while chatting away in his native tongue to another of the crew. Schröder junior I suspected, though my view was obscured by the skipper's cabin. I'd initially assumed that they were father and son until Briggs explained that this was not the case; the crew had adopted the senior/junior suffix as the best way to tell them apart. I suggested that they should simply have been called by their Christian names. However, they had the same problem there as well, apparently. With my rudimentary grasp of the language, I found myself attempting to eavesdrop on their conversation. But with the unrelenting waves battering at the bow and the wind howling through the sails above, another of my senses was left wanting that night.

The ocean, even at her most benevolent, is never the place for quiet contemplation. I'd spent the remaining hours of darkness sitting in my bunk, unable to sleep. A lantern swung hypnotically with the motion of the waves. All around me there was the incessant creaking and cracking of ropes and timber. Above me I could hear the heavy footfalls of other crewmen.

But it wasn't these sounds that kept me from my slumber, but the thought of that distant speck on the horizon. Come first light I'd be topside taking up my duty on watch. I hadn't seen the ship since nightfall. But I knew for certain that come daybreak I'd see her again.

~

As we approached the brig it was obvious to all that she was sitting much lower in the water than would normally be expected. Given how unseaworthy she now appeared to be, I started to doubt that this was the ship I had observed throughout the previous day.

"Easy Mister Gilling, bring her alongside. But not too close, mind," said the skipper. "Mr Briggs, lower the boat."

Briggs nodded to Gorski who was standing at the stern, ready to release the hoist. The whole crew waited silently as the jolly boat was lowered. I kept a steady eye on the brig, trying to determine if we were getting too close. If she were to capsize I didn't want her mainmast striking our deck.

"Persephone," said the skipper, reading the name on the prow. "Anyone recognise the name?"

The crew shook their heads. Dmitry stood back, rolling the pipe in his mouth, looking more sullen by the minute.

It was Schröder junior and, unsurprisingly, me who were elected to accompany the skipper to the brig. I had my reservations about boarding the vessel but, as I was the one who had alerted the crew to the ship's presence, I felt I had a responsibility to be the first to board her.

The remaining crew watched pensively as Schröder rowed the small boat towards the *Persephone.* Schröder senior stood on the quarterdeck slowly paying out the line that I'd tied to the boat. Not knowing what to expect we brought with us two storm lanterns, a sizeable coil of heavy rope and a ladder. I'd taken the opportunity to hook a hatchet to my belt alongside the knife I usually carried. I knew the skipper would have his revolver.

As we neared the brig the sea became much choppier. It was with considerable relief that young Schröder pulled us through. As we bumped along the hull I caught the bulwark with a boathook. The German had already stowed the oars and was beside me with the ladder. He placed this over the rail while I held us as steady as I could. The whole task was made much easier due to the brig's position in the water.

The skipper indicated that I should be the first on deck. Schröder secured the boat as I climbed aboard. I offered a hand to the skipper as he appeared at the railing, while my other hand was beneath my oilskin on the handle of the hatchet.

"Careful, it's slippery underfoot," I nodded to the patches of algae that discoloured the deck.

"It could have been adrift for many weeks," said the skipper as he stepped down. We paused for a moment and waited for Schröder to join us. It was a strange thing for a sailor to board a ship uninvited.

As I have said before, there is no such thing as quiet on a ship. And so it was here. Waves slapped against the hull and the ship would pitch and roll, the timbers creaking and groaning. But here there was something different. Whilst the wind whipped across the deck and lashed us with briny spray, the sound of furiously flapping sails, which was normally so prominent a part of the general cacophony on deck, was eerily absent. It felt akin to standing in a storm-lashed forest in midwinter.

"The sails were cut free," said the skipper as he was examining the ropes trailing from the spars. "They might have been forced to lose the mainsails in a storm, but not all the canvas."

The rest of the deck was in surprisingly good order. The boat was still secured firmly to the deck before the mainmast. A sure sign that whatever had befallen the ship and its crew had been very sudden indeed. Lashed to the base of the mast I noticed two barrels. I walked over to make a closer inspection and bent down to check the contents. By the smell alone I could tell they contained paraffin for refilling the lanterns. I gave the barrels a sharp kick. Each gave a leaden response indicating they were still full.

"They can't have been at sea for more than a day or two when the storm hit them."

Leaving Schröder to keep a weather-eye on deck we directed our attention to the Captain's Cabin. As we entered the skipper pointed out a series of rough furrows gouged into the door. The room beyond looked like any cabin I might happen upon. To one side there was a broad mahogany desk, the top inlayed with leather dyed a deep maroon. The chair beyond it had been overturned and shards of glass from a broken decanter crunched beneath our boots as we entered. Against the far wall a bunk lay unmade, as if its occupant had recently risen.

"I can see nothing too untoward. Or at least nothing that couldn't be blamed on them running into bad weather," said the skipper as he righted the chair.

"What about these?" I asked, running my fingers across the damaged door.

The skipper was checking the desk drawers, obviously looking for something in particular. He glanced up at me, a sly grin playing across his lips.

"Ship's cat?" he said. Then, looking more thoughtful, he sighed.

"This is most peculiar – would you be so kind as to search under the bunk?"

"Aye, skipper. What are we looking for?" I tossed back the covers and then peered beneath the mattress. There was nothing there.

"Look about you, what's missing?"

I glanced about the cramped quarters and instantly understood what the skipper meant. What I had taken to indicate normality was anything but. Where I should have seen charts, scribbled notes and calculations I looked on naught but an empty desk. The tools for the task remained in place, all neatly arranged in a wooden rack on the burgundy top. But anything that might speak to us of the nature and destination of the vessel was missing. From the skipper's reaction I guessed that the drawers were similarly bare.

We left the cabin empty-handed and headed below decks to check the galley and crew's quarters. I lit one of the lanterns we'd brought along and descended the near vertical steps of the ladder that brought us down into the living quarters and into a good two feet of salt water. This finally confirmed our theory of the storm. The light from the lantern glinted on the agitated water and cast freakish shadows about us as we splashed between two of the gently swinging hammocks. At first sight I had thought them to be occupied, but a closer inspection revealed just a tangle of bed-linen.

At the end was the galley and leading to it a large wooden table. I moved slowly in that direction then halted suddenly and took no step closer. The skipper had waded past me, taken the lantern from my hand and carried on forward until the table was between us. Seeing it presented to me in silhouette, the image was even more striking than when I'd first stumbled upon it. For there at the very centre of the table someone had buried, with obvious force and intent, a long hafted axe.

We returned topside more than a little perplexed. Most of the evidence had pointed to this being a case of abandonment in the face of severe weather. The skipper had proposed that the vessel may well have already been unmanned and the storm had blown her without crew or sails into the North Sea. It was a perfectly plausible theory. I would have been more than happy to go along with if it hadn't been for the marks on the door, and the axe.

~

Back on deck I enlisted the assistance of Schröder in opening the hatch that led down into the hold. I had hoped, given how firmly shut it was, that the hold might have been saved from the water flooding the crew's quarters. I was to be disappointed. After several minutes' work we freed the hatch and swung it back to reveal that same noisome stench of brine and stagnation, and our reflected images peering back up at us. If anything the water was deeper in here.

With the boathook in one hand and the lantern in the other I descended into the hold as far as I could. In the constant motion of the sea the polluted water sloshed back and forth, causing little waves to wash over the jumble of cargo and detritus that filled the space. It was like an ocean in miniature. Where the steps met the bilge-water I stopped and used the boathook to try and calculate how high the water had reached. There was at least another five feet. I'd gone as far as I dared. I lowered the lantern to the water to get a better look, holding it out as far as I could without risking pitching myself into the foul liquid. I could see a number of large crates. Most had been disturbed by the treacherous conditions the ship had found herself in. The corners of these boxes jutted out of the water like pyramidal stepping-stones leading to the remaining crates, still tied in neat stacks towards the bow of the brigantine.

All the while I was down there I was relaying every observation I made to the skipper at the hatch overhead. I reached with the hook to the nearest crate and tried to guide it closer. The metal tip caught it and the box slowly turned over as I pulled it towards me. I called for Schröder to take hold of the lantern. I saw his head appear as he bent down and stretched out a hand to meet mine. I then dragged the crate a little closer and seated myself on the lowest dry step to take a better look. I took the hatchet from my belt and slid the blade under the cover of the lid. Very gently I prised it away.

"It appears to be some sort of clay," I called out, withdrawing my hand from the opening and holding it up to the daylight to confirm my diagnosis. "But it's just mud now."

As I was trying to shake the dirt from my hand, something disturbed by my moving the crate drifted up through the slime. I caught it up with the hook and raised it to the light. It was a book.

I squinted up at the hopeful silhouettes peering down into the gloom.

"I've found the logbook," I said and gingerly took hold of the putrid artefact with my free hand and opened it. "Well the cover at least."

I heard the skipper's sigh of disappointment as I thumbed at the torn stubs of the inner pages, then passed the book up to Schröder, who took it with a look of disgust on his face similar to my own.

As I resumed my search in the rippling filth,

perhaps hoping to find some of the torn pages, I sensed a movement above the piled cargo that had not broken free from its fetters. I froze instantly and stared directly ahead. Something was there. Beyond the stack of boxes and the accompanying tangle of securing ropes, that seemed more like the web of an immense spider, I could see what looked like a hunched figure retreating into the farthest shadows of the bulkhead. It must have been my eyes adjusting to the gloom for I hadn't seen anything moments earlier. I took what I saw to be the movement of a man, though I couldn't shake from my mind the image of a spider patiently biding its time. Perhaps my imagination was working against me. For I fear, as I peered into the gloom, I knew I was more than capable of conjuring up a hold full of brigands amongst the shifting shadows.

I called to Schröder to direct the lantern to the recesses of the hold. But before he could do so the ship was rocked by a larger wave. The brig pitched down and then up again, sweeping the bilge water with it. I clambered up the steps as the water washed back. As it settled again I crouched down in order to see back into the hold. But the brief exposure to the daylight had robbed me of my night vision, and whatever I thought I'd seen was again lost in the darkness.

"Mister Gilling, have you found something?" enquired the skipper over Schröder's shoulder. I continued to stare back into the hold as I reached for the ladder.

"I thought I saw something, some..." I turned towards the daylight, could smell the fresh sea air, and felt the oppressive atmosphere dissipate. "It was nothing; just shadows."

I scrambled back onto the deck and found Schröder already preparing to secure the brig to our vessel. The skipper was seated on the upturned hull of the dinghy, holding the remnants of the logbook in his hands. His face was a mask of concentration as if he were trying to conjure the lost pages back, to glean some knowledge where there was none to be had. As I approached him he let the cover fall shut and he tossed the empty book onto the deck.

"What on earth could have happened here?" he wondered aloud.

The crew had attached a heavy rope to the line we had towed across with us. The skipper and I considered our options while the German secured the tow rope to the mast. Ultimately we arrived at two choices: tow her to port with us, or sink her to prevent her becoming a potential problem for any other ships. In truth another heavy storm would probably do for her, and if the weather were to turn against us, none of us would have any qualms about cutting her loose. It was with this thought in mind that the skipper decided against leaving one of the crew on board the *Persephone*. With a favourable wind filling our sails, which we had, there would be no problems pulling the unmanned brigantine smoothly in our wake.

I gave a silent prayer to whatever providence guided the skipper's thinking as I was sure to be the obvious candidate for such a post. The very thought of spending any more time on that accursed ship filled me with a palpable sense of dread. I was, or had always thought of myself as, a rational man. But there was something about this vessel and the manner in which we had encountered it that made me increasingly uneasy. I imagined myself immune to the superstitious nature of most seafarers, and the thought that my mind had in some way been cast adrift from my usual level-headedness troubled me greatly.

It was with immense relief that I was able shut the hatch on the hold full of fouled waters and whatever my imagination had conjured amongst the shadows and return to the *Albin Grau*. I cast a final cursory glance about the deck before heading back to the jolly boat. The skipper and Schröder were already preparing to leave. As I moved to join them my foot caught something. A dark cylindrical object went clattering across the greasy deck. My eye followed the object as it skipped across the weathered planks. It was merely one of the numerous belaying pins used to secure the rigging. I instinctively bent down to pick it up; having such an object loose on a ship's deck could be dangerous indeed. I could see that the pin was damaged and surmised that it had sheared during the storm. It was only as I was returning it to its proper place, in the rail about the mainmast, that I inspected the pin more closely and found that it wasn't broken at all. The tapered end had been deliberately whittled down to a sharpened point.

~

I took second dogwatch that evening. And as the sun started its slow creep towards the horizon, I felt the already chill air drop several degrees further. I blew warm breath into my cupped hands to alleviate the ache in my joints. The icy nor'easter that had announced itself at the start of our voyage reaffirmed its presence and our sails billowed before it. Even with a day lost on the derelict vessel we were still making excellent time. Although my attention should have been on the course ahead, I frequently found myself drawn back to that dark shape that pursued us. *Pursued.* An odd word to choose as the vessel behind us had no choice in the matter, secured to us as she was with a heavy rope.

Was it just the wind that chilled me so? It wasn't only Dmitry that held misgivings about this course of action. But where he had made his feelings clear, I had bitten my tongue. I could offer no rational alternative to towing the vessel. After all we had unusually good weather on our side; with the wind at our backs we were making good time. And with a cargo that wasn't going to spoil, an extra day or so at sea would be more than recompensed with the brig's salvage rights.

Towing a ship the size of the *Persephone* is no small task. We used a heavy tow rope which we attached to the mainmast of the brigantine, by far the strongest part of any ship. The distance between the ships was determined by the wave length; that is to say that the towed vessel would be at least one full peak and trough behind us. This way both ships would rise and fall over the waves together. All told the *Persephone* languished a good hundred yards behind us. But even at this distance it still seemed oppressively close, the naked masts swaying like crosses in a sombre procession.

It was already dark when Nemetz took over the night-watch. Only a sliver of light now separated the starless, leaden sky from the shimmering ocean. And trailing in our wake, straddling the elements of water and air, was the silhouette of the brig, appearing as an inkblot caught between the pages of a book. One page was the sky, the other the sea.

On either side of her prow lanterns glowed. Their flame appeared as red or green through the tinted glass. There was something in their appearance that made me think of my grandfather and the stories he'd tell me as a child.

"Black Shuck," I said aloud, to no-one in particular. Of course Nemetz was standing close by and obviously hearing me, and I felt obliged to explain.

"When I was a young boy, my grandfather would tell stories to my brother and me once we were tucked up in bed. There was one about a huge black dog called Black Shuck that wandered the moors at night. He had fearsome glowing eyes, one red and t'other green.

"It would find some weary traveller or drunkard staggering home from an evening's excess. And then in some lonely place..." I looked up to find the German hanging on my every word.

"And this was to help you sleep?" he asked.

"To keep us in our beds, most as like," I replied.

"And me at my post."

I laughed and nodded towards the vessel behind us. "It was the lanterns on the brig that reminded me of the tale."

Nemetz followed my gaze and we both watched in silence as the two coloured lanterns swung in the impenetrable blackness. As I'd been talking, that final trace of daylight had faded from view and the horizon was lost to us. I recalled the dreams my grandfather's stories would conjure up. Of an immense hound bounding out of the blackest night, its blazing eyes rising and falling with each mighty lolloping stride. I gave an involuntary shiver. The scene before me could have been from that very dream.

"I just hope your Big Shuck behaves himself. At least until Gorski's watch."

It was as Nemetz turned away that I saw the red eye blink. Nemetz hadn't seen it, but I had. The light from the port lantern was briefly extinguished only to suddenly return.

As if an object had passed before it.

I left Nemetz to his watch. Much to his relief I felt, as my rather agitated state was distracting him from his own duties. The *Persephone* followed smoothly in our wake. The two lanterns burned brightly. Everything seemed to be, for want of a better word, shipshape. On the main deck I found Schröder senior and Gorski attending to the sails under Briggs' watchful eye. I could just about see Dmitry on the fo'c'sle deck. He was seated at his favoured position on one of the capstans, pipe all aquiver, his face a mask of concentration as he stared out at an invisible horizon.

"He's still sulking," said Briggs, following my eye line.

"On this I can understand how he feels," I muttered.

"You think the skipper should have left her to drift then?"

"No, the skipper knows best." I'm not sure how convincing that sounded to Briggs as I caught him smile and turn away as I said it.

Briggs, along with the rest of the crew, had listened intently as we recounted what we had discovered aboard the *Persephone*. "So what do you reckon it was then, pox or madness?"

"Storm or not, something else happened on that ship." I wished my own thoughts about the fate of the crew were as mundane as Briggs'. Whenever I turned my mind to such thoughts I found much darker shadows lurking.

"I'll grant you there's summat queer about it."

"You think he might try anything?" I nodded towards the lone figure near the bow.

"Dmitry?" said Briggs looking surprised. "No, he'll complain like there's no tomorrow, cross himself and damn us all for fools and heathens. But he'll toe the line along with the rest of us. There's no-one more dependable than Dmitry. Have no concerns on that count."

It would be hard to imagine Dmitry fitting in comfortably anywhere. He could play the archetypal Russian pessimist to perfection. Like the skipper he had come late to ocean life. As a boy he'd apparently run away from home to join the circus, and toured for many years as part of a trapeze act. I doubted this story myself until I had chance to see how he handled himself about the rigging. He moved with a speed and grace that a sailor half his age would be hard pushed to match. Even Gorski and the younger Schröder were left gawping in amazement. I didn't doubt Dmitry's loyalty but I had concerns over how he might affect the general mood of the crew. I was about to voice this when I heard Nemetz call me from the quarterdeck above.

"Mister Gilling sir, might you spare a moment. There's something you should see."

"What have you seen Nemetz, tell me?" I shouted back, not even bothering to turn around.

I waited for a response, but none came. Or none that I expected. There was a sharp yelp, as one might hear from a dog scolded by its master.

"Nemetz?" I said and started to turn. From my position on the main deck my view of the helm was obstructed. I walked towards the ladder, Briggs in tow.

But it was not Nemetz who answered.

"Kurt!" A voice screamed out from above us.

We both turned to find Gorski scrambling down the ratlines from where he'd been trimming the sails. He landed nimbly on the deck beside us and went haring up the ladder to the quarterdeck. Briggs and I followed with increased urgency. Gorski was already up the ladder as my foot landed on the first step. I looked onto the upper deck to see the Pole running at full pelt to the wheel and come to a sudden halt. But he didn't quite stop. It was akin to seeing someone running into an oncoming wave. I've seen men swatted aside by waves breaking over a ship's bows. But this was no wave.

Gorski was thrown back with incredible force, his body cart-wheeling wildly like some loose-limbed marionette discarded by a petulant child. I lost my footing on the ladder as I made a frantic grab for the stricken sailor. I tumbled backwards, landing heavily on Briggs as Gorski disappeared over the bulwark into the blackness beyond.

The cry of 'man overboard' came from Dmitry as he swung the lifebuoy over the side. But in the darkness there was no way of seeing where Gorski was. I struggled back on my feet and helped a complaining Briggs do the same. The whole crew were now on deck, roused by Dmitry's cry, the skipper included. Everyone besides the first mate and I were immediately engaged in trying to recover Gorski from the water. Their calls into the night went unanswered. The ship was moving at a fair rate of knots, and even a strong swimmer would have only a handful of seconds to reach a lifeline before it would be snatched cruelly away as the ship moved inexorably on. Like most of the crew – and so many sailors I have taken passage with – Gorski was not much of a swimmer.

I remounted the ladder and set off to find out what had happened to Nemetz. As I pulled myself onto the upper deck I saw Nemetz behind the wheel. His legs buckled under him, and he desperately gripped the wooden spokes with one free hand as he slid onto the deck, pulling the wheel round as he fell. His other hand was tucked beneath his chin, his head tipped awkwardly forward as if trying to hold the hand there with his jaw.

As I reached out to him, trying to check his fall and keep our course, I slipped on the wet deck and landed heavily beside him. I looked up into wide, terror-stricken eyes as he dropped towards me. His face and shirt appeared to be blackened, looking like he'd just emerged from the engine room of some modern steamer. I caught the wheel with one hand and let Nemetz fall onto me. I raised myself up slightly as Nemetz fell down into the glare of a lantern that swung from a hook before the wheel. I could see clearly for the first time that it was blood, not oil or grease, covering him. As I held him I could see that I, too, was now daubed with the stuff, having slipped where the blood had started to pool on the deck.

"Nemetz, what in God's name happened?" I said, cradling his head against my forearm.

Quivering lips tried to form words but only pinkish bubbles of saliva issued. He wasn't even looking up at me. He was staring glassy-eyed into the dark; I could see I was losing him. Copious amounts of blood oozed through the fingers that gripped at his throat. I didn't dare remove them for I knew they covered a terrible wound.

I don't remember if it was some movement I detected in the periphery of my own vision or a reflection in Nemetz's dilated eyes, but I found myself turning away from the dying man to where his stare had settled. I nearly dropped the poor sailor onto the hard wooden planks as a tremor of fright surged through me.

At the stern of the ship, no more than a few feet away stood, for want of a more suitable word, a man.

I looked up into a face of a thing that surely inhabited the furthest recesses of what might be called humanity. From the eyes a prominent bony tattooed forehead swept back to a receding hairline. The silver hair hung lankly down, outlining the visage like a gilt frame. The face appeared quite flat, the nose being barely present at all, merely two elongated holes above the upper lip. Like Nemetz and I, he too was bloodied. Rivulets of red ran from the wide slash of a mouth, over the chin, disappearing into the folds of a heavy coat. The figure held both hands out in front; its long nails were reddened and it was rubbing the sticky substance between forefinger and thumb while contemplating its next move.

In the inconstant glow of the swinging lantern the face seemed unnaturally white. The flattened cruel features had raised comparisons to the pale underbelly of a Tope, a shark that inhabits those very same waters. The tattoos that covered the forehead and cheeks, which for all I could guess might continue over the chin and throat beneath that dripping crimson mouth, reminded me of those seen on the brown-skinned faces from the archipelagos of the South Pacific, though the design differed markedly. The fine black marks on that alabaster skin appeared more like those intricate markings scratched by sailors with an hour or two to kill. It looked like scrimshaw on ivory.

And then there were the eyes.

At first it seemed that it possessed none at all. It

was as if I was staring into the empty sockets of a skull. But I did not doubt that these black voids looked back at me. They were the deathless, unblinking eyes of a shark. They were the eyes of a predator.

The figure made as if to advance towards me. I pressed my heels down, trying to find some purchase on the fouled deck. I started to edge back, dragging the prone sailor with me. It was a futile gesture. If the thing fell upon me I knew I was done for.

But the figure made no move in my direction and I could read no change in its demeanour. Instead of attacking it half turned and retreated to the bulwark. I heard a shout from Briggs, who had finally recovered himself and was climbing the ladder. I did not turn to answer his call, but watched dumbstruck as the figure disappeared over the stern in one fluid motion. Briggs came sliding down onto the deck beside me just as the trailing black coat slipped back into the dark space between bulwark and hoisted jolly boat, like a submerging dorsal fin.

"Did you see it?" I said to Briggs as he raised himself.

"I saw... something." The full horror of the situation was just dawning upon him as he saw his own bloodied hands.

"He was attacked," I said before Briggs could ask the question, and nodded towards the stern.

Nemetz started to convulse. He was desperately trying to speak. I lowered my ear closer and could feel the flecks of sputum spatter my cheek.

"Bleichen Hände!" he wheezed in his mother tongue, the words bubbling up through the fluids in his throat. The rest of the crew, led by the skipper, had joined us on the quarterdeck. I looked up to see them crowded around us and I saw the younger Schröder repeat the words, a look of consternation on his face as he glanced up to the elder.

"What did he say?" asked the skipper, his usual brusque tone softened. I noticed he'd even removed his cap.

"Pale hands," I replied.

Nemetz grabbed tightly at the sleeve of my coat and tried to lift himself up. I turned to calm him. His eyes were locked on me as if I held within me some means to assist in his survival or, perhaps, his salvation.

"Shuck," he whispered to me. I felt his grip relax as he said it and I knew he was gone. I let the body slide from me and tried to get back on my feet. I do not know if anyone else caught that final word, but I alone understood what the word meant and felt its chill.

"I saw who did this," I said to the skipper as he helped me stand. He gave a look of surprise as if it hadn't occurred to him that another party had been involved. Before he could ask me what I meant, Briggs spoke up. He was standing at the stern, his back to all of us. On first seeing him I thought the surfeit of blood had been too much for him to stomach.

"I see him still," he said and pointed along the tow rope towards the brig.

We looked along the thick rope to where Briggs directed our gaze. At first I could see nothing. The rope stretched out into the darkness and was consumed by the black shape of the *Persephone*. Then, as my eyes adjusted to the distance and dark, I saw a movement, a shadow amongst the broader abstracts of ship and sea.

From the gasps around me I knew I was not the only witness. Two thirds of the way along the tow rope a figure, that might be a man, moved with surprising swiftness. With legs hooked over the rope and using a hand-over-hand motion the figure crossed the water between the two ships with apparent ease. The bulk of the figure disappeared into shadow as it neared the brig, leaving only the pale hands visible. The grey flesh might so easily have been mistaken for rats, or possibly hopping gulls. *Pale hands*. Nemetz had seen their approach. If I'd responded sooner might he have yet lived, or would I be lying with him on that blood-streaked deck?

I turned away from the brig and, conscious of the body still sprawled on the deck, tried to avoid making contact with its glassy stare. I stumbled into Dmitry who had been standing directly behind me. I tottered back from him, a feeling of sickness overwhelming me. My face and hands felt constricted where the blood was starting to dry. He looked down on me, the bone pipe immobile in that grimly clenched jaw, my head swimming as I raised myself up to meet his gaze.

"I think you need to clean yourself up, Mister Gilling," he said as he stepped aside to let me pass. I could feel his eyes on me as I staggered below decks.

~

It was the appearance of a sombre glow on the horizon that marked an end to that terrible night. No one had slept and we all nervously paced the deck while keeping a vigilant watch on the *Persephone*. We had armed ourselves with whatever weapon we could find and the deck was illuminated with a dozen storm lanterns. Whether through fear of another visitation from Nemetz's attacker or the reluctance of sharing space with his corpse, lying below decks wrapped in canvas sheets, I cannot say.

Throughout the night we'd argued about the best course of action open to us. None of us were foolish enough to suggest we attempt anything until the morning. So there we huddled like helpless seals on an ice floe waiting for that grey dawn.

For my part I'd described what I had seen, though now that I was removed from any imminent threat I found that my impression of the man who had killed Nemetz and hurled Gorski to certain death sounded too fanciful to be believed. Briggs, who arrived after me, did nothing to contradict what I said, but offered little by way of corroboration, either. As the interrogation developed I found myself thinking that what I had seen was merely a man and anything more I bestowed upon him was a product of my own shocked and disordered mind.

Only Dmitry remained silent during this questioning, and throughout he observed me with a thoughtful countenance. He finally spoke up when the question of what was to be done came up.

"Cut her adrift," he addressed the skipper directly. "We have lost two fine men this night. We must do what is right for the ship."

Quite when these two unfortunates became fine

men in Dmitry's eyes I do not know, but there was no doubting the passion with which he bolstered his argument.

"What is right for the ship is my concern," replied the skipper, meeting the eyes of all the crew assembled there. Perhaps he felt a growing support for Dmitry's view of the situation and had decided to reclaim his authority.

"My loyalties are to the ship and its owners, to our cargo and only then to its crew. The crew are the most expendable of all these things. That is the law of the sea and you all set your mark to it." He paused, gauging the reaction, watching Dmitry closest of all. "Persons not known to us have boarded my ship, killed two of my crew, and you think I shall stand by and let this outrage pass unpunished? I will have this fiend captured and put in irons or dead by my own hand. At first light we shall board the *Persephone* and deal with this unwelcome passenger. Justice, gentlemen, is the one thing I will place above all others."

None of us, Dmitry included, could have doubted his sincerity. The skipper was a man of uncommon calmness, even in the most fraught of conditions. A godsend when you're riding into an oncoming gale and the spindrift is whipped from the cresting waves, threatening to overwhelm you. But there were occasions when such a placid demeanour seemed to be misplaced. Of course the skipper hadn't seen what I had; no man who had looked on that face would actively seek it out again. Perhaps I should have spoken out – if I'd thrown my hat in with Dmitry... but where would that have brought us? I shook the thought from my head, even though I would never dare to articulate such ideas, as I knew them to be mutinous and unworthy of me. It was Briggs who told me when we first shipped out of Wismar that the skipper subscribed to some new philosophical movement called *The Pragmatics*.

One way or another, it seems, the sea makes philosophers of us all.

~

The cold grey light of morning brought back memories of the previous night. The quarterdeck still bore the stains missed by the younger Schröder's hurried night time clean-up. Even that bitter, brine-flecked wind failed to chase away the copperish scent of blood that assailed my nostrils as I came up the ladder. I stepped onto the deck and cast a sideways glance to where Gorski had been pitched headlong into the water. Amidst the turbulent foam washed from the hull I could still see the trailing lifelines cast out to the unfortunate sailor.

"Skipper's invited me on his little expedition, so that'll leave you to keep on eye on things here," said Briggs as I reached the stern. He was overseeing the loading of the boat. Beside us the German sailors were hefting a portable bilge-pump into the craft. "You don't mind?"

I was too focused on trying to hide my relief at this news to give him any meaningful response. As chief witness to last night's events I naturally assumed I'd be first in line to join the boarding party. I'd spent most of the night pacing about the deck with that one thought preying on my mind: that I would have to face that thing again.

"I'm sure the skipper knows best," I replied, looking at the brig that cut relentlessly through our wake. The square-rigged mast stood out starkly against the brightening eastern sky. It wasn't a procession I saw now, but a tiny wooden hill of crosses. We were pulling our own private Golgotha with us. Everything I saw, thought or said had become infused with portent.

"You'll be keeping Dmitry company," said Briggs.

"Really? I'd have thought the skipper would have wanted to keep a closer eye on him."

"I think it's more about keeping him out of the way, after last night."

I found our conversation returning to where it had been left hanging the night before.

"Still, isn't the skipper showing some faith in Dmitry by leaving him here?"

"And in you also," he replied and turned away, leaving me to ponder the significance those last words.

~

"Do what you must, but be done by nightfall."

These words were Dmitry's as he untied the jolly boat and watched it drift away from us. The schooner remained under light sail so our journey home continued, if somewhat slower than might be anticipated. The Russian slowly payed out the line to the little boat as it pitched and rolled through the disturbed waters of our wake towards the *Persephone*. Approaching any vessel this way would seem a foolhardy proposition, and more than once I thought they would be overwhelmed or capsized by the ferocity of the water breaking against her bow. But with Dmitry feeding out the rope with a steady hand, Schröder needed do no more that keep the craft steady and avoid being dragged too close to the prow.

We both held our breath as the boat slid alongside the brig. I'd watched the whole endeavour through the telescope and could clearly see Briggs take a firm hold on the ship with the boathook. Once we saw that the boat was secured, my attention returned to the helm of the schooner.

I kept her on an even steady course while always on the lookout for any approaching weather fronts. Dmitry watched the activity on the brig as the crew prepared to search the vessel.

"You think that it was just a man that you saw here last night, Mister Gilling?"

Dmitry had finally chosen his moment to speak. I sensed he'd been waiting for the opportunity all morning.

I turned to find him still looking across to the brig, but I could not help but notice that he stood on the very spot I had seen what we now called 'our passenger'.

"Of course it was a man," I replied, slightly thrown by the question. Dmitry's position on the deck had already brought the image of the thing back to me, "though he seemed to be deformed or diseased in some way. Leprous."

Who was I trying to convince – Dmitry or myself?

"Leprous," he repeated and let the word hang for a moment. "You think a leper could have crawled with such ease along this rope?"

I looked back at the tow rope, the distance seeming so great it was all but invisible before it reached the *Persephone*.

"I did not say he was a leper; but what I saw looked like a man."

Dmitry just nodded but didn't answer. He then looked at me as if something had just occurred to him.

"I'd hoped that no one else had seen the ship," he said. His rough accent rendered each word as a despondent growl.

"You saw it and said nothing?"

"As did you; for a time at least."

My apprehension over the appearance of the brig had been supplanted by the events of the previous evening.

"You knew something of this vessel?" I asked.

Dmitry shook his head. "I spotted her as we entered open water. I think you did too. At first I saw nothing that troubled me. A ship without sails so far from land is strange, but without a distress signal it was not a concern for Dmitry. It was only as she came about as we sailed past I felt something was wrong."

"But this cannot have been the *Persephone*. Even allowing for the vagaries of ocean currents, she couldn't have kept pace with us." It wasn't for Dmitry's benefit that I argued thus. Any attempt to rationalise with the Russian was a lost cause. What he said had confirmed everything I had feared all along, and I did not welcome hearing it.

"It depended on us spotting her and being curious enough to board. If we had carried on we would, at length, have escaped, and then she would have waited for another ship to be lured to her."

"But this is ridiculous, what you're suggesting makes no sense."

"You want sense, Mister Gilling?" I could see Dmitry warming up to the argument. Briggs had warned me against getting involved in such a discussion. "Here we are bobbing along all alone in this insignificant little boat. In every direction there is nothing. Look."

He gestured to all points of the compass, then up to the sky and into the surging waters. "You see there is nothing. If it's some sense of reason you're after then you are not going to find it out here."

"I've sailed as far and as wide as you, Dmitry, and have seen much that defies belief, but I have never looked to the supernatural for an explanation." I tempered the tone of agitation in my voice. I really didn't want us coming to blows.

"I'm not about to question your experience, Mister Gilling. When our saviour walked into the wilderness, he entered it alone. This is our wilderness, and we are all beyond God's grace here." His tone instantly softened. "Don't you believe in God?"

His sudden change of tack caught me and I found myself without an adequate reply. I had no idea where this conversation was going, but I was damned sure I wouldn't be kneeling in Nemetz's bloodstains, praying alongside Dmitry for a safe passage home. "That is really none of your concern."

I turned my back to the Russian and looked to the other vessel. I placed a hand on the rope that held the brig. But in Dmitry's mind it was the *Persephone* that had a hold on us. Though the *Persephone* was the smaller of the two vessels, she seemed to have grown in stature; appearing so much closer now than she had last night. Was this some trick of the light, or was she slowly reeling us in?

Her ragged naked masts jutted defiantly towards the heavens. If the sun had broken free of the cloud cover, I feared that the shadow cast would have easily bridged the distance between us and fallen across our deck like a grasping hand. I couldn't help but picture her as a spider upon a shimmering web. That web was the ocean.

Activity on the *Persephone* caught my attention and lifted me from my reverie. I watched as a plume of greenish water erupted over the side of the brig. The portable bilge-pump was finally engaged in emptying the flooded hold. This was soon joined by another jet of water. The ship's own pump was still working; this would without doubt hasten the operation, though clearing the hold of so much water would take them well into the afternoon.

We both watched in silence at the first real signs of progress from the other ship. Dmitry looked pensive, the ivory pipe gripped firmly between yellowed teeth. He would occasionally glance up at the bright spot on the silver grey pall of cloud. I too felt an increasing sense of helplessness as I followed the sun on its inexorable trajectory.

~

"So tell me Dmitry," I finally broke the uneasy silence that had settled over us as we kept our distant watch on the brig. "Who do you think it was that killed poor Nemetz and Gorski?"

"There are..." he paused for a moment as if searching for a suitable word and, I suspect, failing to do so, "men who would inhabit the lonelier places of the world. They shun humanity because they are no longer part of it."

"And you have encountered these... men?

Dmitry shook his head. "No, but I have looked into the faces of those who have and that is enough to know the truth of it."

"I think I would need more proof."

"Be careful what you wish for, Mister Gilling."

"But for anyone to exist out here?" I swept my arm out, gesturing to the massive expanse of water. I considered the choice of words I had spoken. *To exist?* I meant survive, surely?

"Every beast has its own hunting ground. For the wolf it is the forest; for the shark it is the ocean," answered Dmitry. Still he avoided applying a name, as if doing so would act as a kind of invocation. "I can see it in your eyes Mister Gilling – you think that Dmitry is a superstitious old fool."

In truth a part of me did think this, even as my head shook in denial. But there was one thing that had kept me from dismissing all that Dmitry spoke of out of hand.

"I might have thought such a thing, if it were you alone who had put such ideas into my head. This hardly counts as proof but there is something I want you to see." Retrieving it from my coat, I held out the sharpened belaying pin so Dmitry could see it clearly. "I found this lying on the deck of the *Persephone*."

Dmitry visibly shuddered at the sight of the whittled point, and for a moment I expected him to cross himself. I think that Dmitry wanted to be proved wrong, secretly hoping that I could assuage his more outlandish thoughts. Instead it looked as though I'd confirmed his worst fears, and in doing so confirmed my own.

"Did the skipper see it, also?

I shook my head. "No-one else; I slipped it into

my coat pocket as we disembarked. It didn't seem so important then."

"And now?"

"I have looked into the face of the thing that slew Nemetz. Tell me Dmitry – what truth do you see in me?"

"Still you won't accept what it is we face." He searched my countenance for some clues to my inner thoughts.

"I dare not believe it."

~

On the *Persephone* the water being pumped from below decks had become a trickle. We watched as the crew disappeared from sight to commence their search through the cargo hold.

Dmitry cast an eye skywards. "They've only got a few hours before it starts to get dark."

We returned to our silent vigil on the deck. The stays buzzed, the sails rippled. I looked up pensively at the grey clouds; the wind was changing direction, taking with it our run of luck with the weather. Two men might hold a ship on course in calm conditions, but if a gale blew up we'd most likely end up like the ship we were towing.

The thought shocked me. Were we unwittingly re-enacting the fate of the crew of that ship? I was about to voice my concerns to Dmitry when I noticed movement on the brig. Through the telescope I saw the skipper appear on the deck, followed by Briggs. They conversed for a few moments then Briggs looked over to me and waved. I returned the gesture but could see from his and the skipper's demeanour that their search had not been a success.

Briggs indicated that they would be returning presently, before disappearing below again to assist in bringing up the equipment. It was not before time, as I noted that the light was already beginning to fail, exacerbated by an advancing weather front that loomed menacingly on the horizon. Now only the skipper remained on deck, seating himself on the upturned hull of the dinghy. He did not once look in our direction, but appeared lost in other thoughts.

My own relief was tempered by a single thought that I'm sure was shared by all. What had become of our unwelcome passenger? I did wonder if the creature had, fortuitously for us, fallen into the sea as it had retreated to the brig. Though the agility it had shown made me think it unlikely that it might have perished as Gorski had done. But there was another possibility – I cast a glance along the empty ship and felt a chill run the length of my spine.

"Dmitry, was a watch kept on the brig all last night?"

"I kept watch until first light," he nodded, eyeing me suspiciously. Perhaps aware of where my question was leading.

"Is it possible that our passenger might have returned? Amid the chaos of last night and still under the cover of darkness it might have crept back onboard. It must have known that we would pursue it come the morning."

Dmitry looked doubtful.

"But what better place to hide?" Again it was the fate of the brig's crew that was foremost in my mind. "Have we been looking on the wrong ship all along?"

"I do not think it would have taken such a risk," said Dmitry. "But there is only one way to be sure."

Neither of us had ventured below since the others had boarded the *Persephone*. I think that neither of us had the stomach to face the shrouded corpse of Nemetz that lay there, the only stillness in the rolling, creaking dark. But now perhaps there was something else waiting, listening to our foolish chatter with a vicious grin spreading across its pallid lips. I did not expect Dmitry to take on the task, that should be mine alone. I tied off the wheel and picked up one of the lanterns from the deck. Dmitry caught my arm as I made for the ladder.

"I think it would be better if I go," he said.

"Nonsense man, I'm quite capable of dealing with this myself," I replied.

"I don't doubt it, and in any other circumstance would be happy to let you go, but you are not as expendable as I. As the skipper himself said, it should be in the interests of the ship and its cargo that we should act first."

He took the lantern from me without further protest.

"Here, take this with you," I said and offered him the belaying pin.

He looked at it quizzically, as if weighing up its usefulness as a weapon, before taking it from me with a curt nod of gratitude. He tucked it into his belt and descended the ladder, muttering what I took to be a prayer.

On the *Persephone* the deck now appeared to be empty. I'd hoped they'd have finished by now. Even in the time that had passed since I'd last seen the skipper it had become noticeably darker. I opened the telescope and surveyed the deck. At first I saw nothing. Then a darker shape appeared against the upturned keel of the dinghy. I started slightly and lost sight of the thing. I centred the glass back onto the dinghy, my heart rising up into my tightening throat. I let out a sigh of relief as I saw it was the skipper. But what was he doing? He was leaning against the boat, his head cocked slightly as if listening to something. Again the blood thundered in me. Something was wrong.

The skipper stepped back and appeared to call out, though from this distance I couldn't hear his words as the wind snatched them away. I lowered the glass and could see the young German clamber onto the deck holding an axe. As he approached the skipper the dinghy between them shook violently. The previous day I had seen it up close and had observed that it was securely tethered to the deck. Now it was not. The skipper stumbled back as a second tremor shook the dinghy. This time it was flipped up into the air. For a moment it seemed to hang above them as it turned over and I watched in horror as the skipper, unable to retreat further back, was crushed against the bulwark as the dinghy came crashing down on him.

"Dmitry!" I screamed, not daring to turn away from the terrible spectacle unfolding before me. I returned the glass to my eye and could see Schröder retreating back to the hold, the axe held defensively before him. I looked to where the skipper had been standing, but now all I could see was the upended dinghy and I feared the poor skipper crushed to death beneath it. In the space that the boat had vacated there was what at first glance appeared to be a dark conical shape, partially obscured by the foremast. I knew at once that it was our passenger.

He threw back the long black coat covering him and stood fully erect before the quaking Schröder. The figure kept his back to me so I was unable to see the face. Whether it just regarded Schröder silently, as it had me, or attempted some form of communication, I cannot say. But the German obviously panicked and flung the axe at the figure. It was poorly aimed and narrowly missed the intended target. The figure barely flinched as the weapon flew past it. Having thus disarmed himself, Schröder turned and fled back, running straight into the arms of Briggs and the elder German, who had just appeared amidships.

"Dmitry! God dammit man, where are you?"

"I hear you, I am..." His voice trailed off as he came up the ladder. Even as he looked past me towards the brig, I observed that there was already a pallid cast to his countenance. His face had the sheen of someone in the midst of a flux. He was evidently not prepared for the sight that greeted him, and the small whale-bone pipe slipped from his mouth and clattered to the deck.

In the failing light we could see Briggs and the two remaining sailors retreating along the deck. Either Briggs or Schröder had brought up a lantern from below. This illuminated our shipmates but rendered the other presence a silhouette. It began to advance on them.

"You were right all along, Dmitry," I said as we both watched helplessly.

"Was I?" he replied.

His response struck me as strange but I ignored it. "If they can get to the boat we can pull them to safety."

I pointed to the small boat that bobbed against the brig's hull.

"I think they may have left it too late."

This was true. Already the passenger had not only advanced on them, but had crossed the deck, putting himself between our crew and their only means of escape.

"I could try a shot," I said looking to the rifle leaning against the winch. "But at this distance I'm as likely to hit one of our own, if I hit anything at all."

I could see it might be our one remaining hope and took up the rifle.

"You will not kill it," growled the voice beside me, sounding like Dmitry of old.

"I'll be lucky to get that close," I said, sighting my target with my good eye and gently squeezing the trigger. "I just need to distract it."

There was a sharp crack as I fired. Taking into account distance and wind-speed, I'd aimed to hit my target squarely in the back. However, I saw no reaction and surmised that my shot had gone wide.

I quickly reloaded and found my target again. Another shot rang out. It was still some way off but it had the desired effect. The bullet caught the foremast, sending out a shower of splintered wood. The creature spun round, looking first at the damaged mast then across the foaming wake to where I stood, rifle in hand.

Briggs saw his chance and rushed the distracted figure, the axe he held aloft glinting in the lantern's glow. The creature started to turn, but Briggs brought the axe down hard. It bit deep into the left shoulder blade. It was a blow that would have felled any man in an instant. But this, as Dmitry had said, was not a man. It continued to turn unabated, and with a flailing arm it swiped at Briggs, the long nails raking through the heavy coat. It sent him reeling back towards his crew mates, clutching with bloodied hands the wound to his breast. We could do nothing but look on, impotent and despairing, as the thing commenced its advance – the haft of the axe still protruding from its shoulder like a single malformed wing.

Dmitry picked up an axe and stepped up to the tow rope.

"What do you think you're doing?" I shouted, seeing the look of determination in him. It was the first time I'd looked directly at him since his return from below deck. The sleeves of his shirt revealed traces of blood; his hands were similarly spattered.

"Good God man, are you injured?" I stared aghast.

"It is nothing, I am not hurt," he reply was dismissive.

"What happened?"

He stared at his stained hands as if surprised to find them thus. "I heard you call and in the rush I missed my footing on the step. That is all."

I didn't believe him – there was no-one more sure-footed than Dmitry. But I could see he was keen that I cease this line of questioning.

"If we cut ourselves free, can we not then sail her about and board the ship?"

I tried to comprehend what the Russian was proposing, so swiftly had he changed the subject, and almost laughed at so ridiculous an idea. He was clutching at straws and we both knew it.

"With a full crew then, yes, perhaps we could. But..." I looked to the rope that still held the jolly boat. Dmitry followed my eye, rushed over to the rope and tugged at it firmly. It showed no signs of giving; Schröder had tethered the boat securely. He tested the rope a few more times, aware that he might tear the lifeline from the boat itself. He finally gave up and threw his head into his hands, howling in frustration.

The solitary lantern lay on the deck of the *Persephone*. As the flame guttered in the strengthening wind, the skeletal rigging seemed to dance about the mast as if it were some May Day celebration. Apart from the dinghy the deck was now empty. I could see no sign of our crew or the creature.

"I didn't see where they went," I said.

Dmitry appeared at my shoulder rubbing at his eyes with his palms. He squinted at the brig. "They must have retreated to the galley. If it is as you described to me, they may try to hold the fiend at bay, for a while at least."

"Until daybreak?"

"Not very likely," said Dmitry. "They may be dead already. Even if they have light down there, which I doubt," he pointed to the solitary lantern flickering in the darkness, "they will be no match for the creature. Now we have to look to our own survival, there is unfinished business."

Dmitry again took up the axe leaning up beside the wheel. He tested the blade with his thumb, feeling its keenness.

"I cannot allow you to do this."

"It will come for us next, you do realise that don't you, Mister Gilling?"

I nodded. "We cannot abandon them, not if there is still hope."

"There is no hope. Not for them, and once it has finished its business on that cursed vessel there shall be none for us, unless we act decisively."

Dmitry made a move towards the tow rope. I caught his arm and he turned to me, his grip tightening on the axe. It was clear that if it came to a fight the Russian had me at a disadvantage. I looked over to where I'd cast the rifle. I released my hold on Dmitry and took a step sideways towards it.

"I cannot allow you to cut them adrift, even if it risks our own lives. If the skipper and first mate are indeed both dead, then their responsibilities fall to me."

Dmitry stopped, and he too glanced at the fallen weapon I was slowly edging towards and laughed. "You think me a mutineer? No, I now concede that the skipper was right all along. We cannot just cut her loose for other unfortunates much like ourselves to stumble upon. No, we must destroy the *Persephone*, along with her passenger. It is not only our lives that are at stake here, but our very souls."

Dmitry tied a lifeline around his waist, then tucked the axe into his belt and took a hold of the tow rope. He looked down into turbulent waters at the stern. He hesitated for a moment, as if his resolve was about to fail him. He took a deep breath and, using the winch as support, climbed onto the bulwark and took a firm hold of the rope in both hands.

"Keep a watch over me and don't let the line get too loose," he said. "If you see anything give the line a firm tug. But not too hard as I'm not much of a swimmer."

"This is madness," I said, taking the lifeline. I looked out to where the tow rope narrowed to a hairline almost invisible in the gloom. "It's much too far. Surely there must be some other way?"

Dmitry shook his head. "If he can do it then so shall Dmitry." He had to shout now to be heard as the wind buffeted him. He leaned out over the roiling sea. Another deep breath and he swung both legs up to the rope and crossed both heels. Hanging thus he slowly pulled himself along. As soon as he left the relative shelter that the schooner offered he was lashed by the wind. The crashing waves beneath seemed to reach up and attempt to pluck him from the rope with spindrift fingers. Dmitry paused for a moment, to get a measure on the elements railing against him. Then after regaining his composure he started moving again, employing that same deliberate hand-over-hand technique adopted by the creature – though Dmitry couldn't hope to match its speed.

After several minutes Dmitry neared the *Persephone*. I conscientiously payed out the line while keeping a close watch on the man and his destination. The lantern on the main deck was the only source of light available as darkness closed in. It was as a silhouette against this light that I saw the bulky form of the Russian finally slip down from the rope onto the deck. After a minute or two of waiting while Dmitry regained his breath, I felt the line in my hand slacken as he released himself. I extended the telescope and watched as the sailor stole across the deck towards where the dinghy lay. It rocked back and forth with the movement of the sea and I shuddered to think of the poor skipper crushed beneath it, like grain on a quern stone.

Sickened by my thoughts of the sights that now faced Dmitry, I looked away. My eye fell on the rifle that still lay where I had cast it earlier. I retrieved the weapon and fished out a shell from the handful that jingled in my coat pocket. I ejected the spent casing, loaded the shell into the breach and returned to my favoured position at the stern. I took up the telescope and looked for Dmitry. At first I could see nothing – the glare from the lantern seemed to render the darker parts of the brig even more impenetrable.

The lantern suddenly dimmed. I let the glass fall from my eye thinking that the light had been extinguished. The light returned just as quickly as

I observed Dmitry move stealthily along the deck. He adopted the sloped shoulder posture of someone prepared to duck out of sight at the first sign of danger. I watched as he passed by the lantern and disappeared. He was heading to either the cabin or crew's quarters.

"What are you doing, Dmitry?" I said, while focussing the telescope on the place I'd last seen him. I then sought out the captain's cabin. I found the pale scratches on the closed door. They looked to me now more like the marks placed at the threshold to a plague-ridden house. The ship's masts denied me a clear view, so I moved my attention to the edge of the raised hatchway where both doors stood wide open. It was here that Dmitry had slipped from my sight. I concentrated only on what I could see through that narrow tube, everything outside its confines ceased to matter. Any minute now Dmitry – *dear God let it be Dmitry!* – would appear. The lantern flickered, harried by the gusting winds, and set the shadows around the hatchway dancing. A fragile ghost of that flame hung inverted within the optics of my glass. I struggled to keep a bead on the pitching deck as both ships rose and fell amidst the battling seas. Still nothing emerged. My free hand fumbled for the rifle – I had to be ready. I let my hand slide along the stock until I found the trigger.

Something moved. I tried to follow with the telescope but lost sight immediately. I dropped the glass from my eye and watched the figure come bounding out of the hatch. It came around the mainmast and, without stopping, took up the lantern from the deck. I watched as the lantern was swung wildly about as the figure came around the open hold along the starboard side of the deck. As it reached the place where the dinghy had once rested it stopped and turned. There was a moment's hesitation and I saw Dmitry, for thank God it was he, swing the lantern upwards. He held it there as if waiting for a command. Then he dashed it down onto the deck.

Like the imprisoned djinn finally released from its bottle the small flame leapt across the deck and up the mast in a rolling, triumphal ball of flame. No single lantern could have done this. The whole midsection of the ship was now fully ablaze. Now I saw what Dmitry had planned for the *Persephone*. Using the barrels of paraffin, he had dowsed the deck and no doubt poured plenty below for good measure.

Dmitry had the good sense not to stop and admire his handiwork. He ran over to the side of the ship and scrambled down into the waiting jolly boat. I was already at the line to pull him to safety. As the vessel pitched about the burning oil was washed over the remaining deck. From the scuppers dotted around the bulwark I could see the burning liquid dripping into the clamouring waves like molten gold. Soon nothing would remain that would justify calling her a ship. She was a bonfire.

The Russian had untethered the boat and I began to haul on the rope. Dmitry, determined not to leave me with all the work, took up both oars and battled through the storm-lashed wake of the schooner. The all-consuming fire lit up the sea between the two ships. It shimmered like a seam of quartz in a coal face. Then my eye was caught by something that looked like sparks cascading from a smithy's anvil. It was only as they splashed into the water that I realised they were rats, their fur aflame. But no rat would ever run into fire, unless driven through it.

Dmitry must have seen it before I did, for he suddenly started to row more frantically. I followed the path the rats had taken through the fire and there I saw a plume of flame rise up and move against the wind towards the prow. At first my mind would not allow me to accept that the shape of it corresponded to that of a man. It was only as it stepped from the wall of flame and started to divest itself of the burning garments that I could see it for what it was.

It came crawling along the bowsprit, naked

now, the human characteristics more difficult to apply. The long, thin, twisted limbs gave no hint to the strength that I had seen them possess. I had on many an unhappy occasion witnessed the effects that malnutrition can do to the body. What I saw in this creature reminded me of the corpses of sailors who had succumbed to a slow starvation.

The head appeared too large; the tangled lengths of hair that had framed the terrible face were now reduced to burnt clumps. The flattened face with its expressionless mouth and empty eyes remained unchanged. The curious drawings that covered the face continued down the torso and arms. The marbled flesh, jaundiced by the firelight, was blackened and sore where the clothing had offered least protection. Open wounds on the creature's stomach and thigh glistened through the burnt skin that curled about the edges like wood shavings.

At the end of the spar it hesitated. Its gaze followed the small boat that was already halfway between the two vessels. A motionless silhouette against the inferno, it made for a macabre figurehead. It would have been better suited to peering from the lofty heights of a cathedral.

I realised my mistake the moment the creature rose from its crouched pose on the bowsprit. Before I went to assist the Russian I should have cut loose the tow rope. I glanced up at the heavy umbilical that connected the ships. I cursed it and myself, but the fire that ravaged the *Persephone* had yet to take a hold of the rope. Even as I thought this I saw that pale grotesque leap up and, as if totally untroubled by the wounds it had suffered, coil itself about the rope and start towards me. As it scrambled onto the line I saw the vicious cut that Briggs had delivered to the creature's shoulder with the axe. The skin parted with the strain put upon it and I could imagine white bone glinting like bared teeth within that terrible wound. I knew that if I didn't act quickly then I, too, would be joining my unfortunate friend.

Uninhibited by any need for caution now and desperate to flee from its burning home, the creature moved along the rope with astonishing speed. I leapt to the tow rope trailing the line to Dmitry behind me. The Russian, having seen the figure advancing on him, rowed ever more frantically; I could see that the gap between them was closing fast. The creature's path, unhindered by the turmoil that Dmitry faced below, came swiftly onwards, hand over hand. It moved with a strange fluidity that seemed almost hypnotic and I imagined this was how Nemetz had first seen it coming at him out of the dark. But now it no longer possessed, nor needed, a reason to hide within the shadows. There was a strange choreography to those slender ravaged limbs, with their angular jabbing joints, that carried it along the rope. The image I had conjured up a few scant hours earlier of a spider upon its web was now horribly brought to life.

I took up my hatchet, and with a firm hold on the rope, I swung the blade down upon it. The small hatchet bit deep into one of the strands and the rope bucked away from my grip. But I had not severed it. Oh, what I would have given for the axe Dmitry had taken. I could not bring myself to look at it fully but I caught in my peripheral vision a momentary hesitation from the advancing thing. The blow had resonated along the rope and it knew what my intentions were. In raising the hatchet a second time, I let the line to Dmitry slip from me. It dropped to the deck and instantly snaked away from my grasping hand. I saw the creature start advancing again. With barely thirty yards remaining, Dmitry would have to wait.

I struck the rope again and it gave some more. A third time and two of the strands broke loose and unravelled. The two remaining braided strands creaked in protest at the weight they alone bore. One final blow would be enough. I swung the hatchet and, as the blade cut into the rope, I looked at the thing and I saw that it had already stopped in its advance and now hung below the rope with arms extended as if resigned to whatever fate the final blow would bring.

There was a loud crack and a shower of fibres as the rope failed. I jumped aside as the severed end was whipped away from me. The creature waited until the final moment. As the rope above it slackened and started to coil about, the creature let go. It had failed to reach the ship, but it had come far enough.

It had caught up with Dmitry.

I felt a knot of despair tighten in my stomach and looked on helplessly as the figure dropped down onto the little boat below. Dmitry had seen it coming and had hurled himself towards the bow as the thing landed heavily. He freed one of the oars from its lock and brandished it towards the tangle of pale limbs that slowly unfolded before him.

Our distance from the burning ship continued to grow, robbing me of the only viable source of light. I scrambled about the deck and found the trailing line to the jolly boat. With Dmitry no longer rowing this, too, was drifting away in the wake of the schooner. The Russian was successfully keeping the thing at oar's length, but I knew that stalemate wouldn't last much longer. The little boat bounced along in our wake, buffeted on both sides by wave and wind. If Dmitry lost his footing he was almost certainly done for.

I tied off the line and retrieved the rifle. I fumbled through my coat pockets and found three unspent cartridges. I moved quickly yet cautiously, not wishing to alert the creature to my endeavours. Taking up a lifebuoy, I lowered it carefully over the stern of the ship, then payed out the line until I could see it bobbing through the water several feet before the jolly boat. I knew I could not bring Dmitry any closer with that thing still on board. But if he could reach the buoy then the creature would be stranded. From what I had already witnessed I fancied that the fiend, for whatever reason, preferred not to get wet. Knowing of many of my own kind's fear of treading open water it may once have been a sailor in some previous existence.

"Dmitry!" I called out. Even above the cacophony of wind and wave I was sure that he would hear, though he did not turn round. "Grab the buoy, it's the only way."

I saw him lash out with the oar and as he did so he glanced back towards the buoy and I knew for sure that he'd understood. The creature nonchalantly battered away the wooden blade as if it was toying with the man. I realised that Dmitry had become a sort of hostage. It knew that while Dmitry lived, I was powerless to act against it. As I raised the rifle and centred the monster in my sights, it was this certainty that I was relying upon.

I squeezed the trigger and felt the gun buck in my hands. From my slightly elevated vantage point I had a clear enough shot at the pale upper torso. I saw it stumble back and knew I'd found my mark. Dmitry turned and scrambled forward, preparing to hurl himself from the boat. Even as I ejected the spent casing and reloaded the creature had regained its footing and lashed out at the fleeing sailor. Dmitry rolled to the side and swung up with the oar to counter the attack. The creature grabbed the oar and wrenched it from the Russian's hand. I was about to fire my second shot as the creature fell upon the stricken sailor. It caught him up in a horrible embrace and dragged him back down into the boat. I could see Dmitry fighting to keep the fiend at arms length, but the distance between them was to narrow for me to chance another shot.

"For God's sake Dmitry, get its head up," I hissed to myself, trying to distinguish friend from foe.

As if in answer to me, the beast suddenly reared up, blood smeared about the cruel slit of its mouth. Whether Dmitry had found some untapped reserve of strength or the thing rose up in exaltation over its fallen prey I cannot say. But it was the opportunity I'd been waiting for.

There came a sharp crack of the report and the creature tumbled back. Even amidst the unrelenting waves it was a shot I could not, dare not, miss. I'd aimed squarely at the large forehead and from the violence with which the creature was flung back, I judged I'd hit it pretty close. I instantly reloaded, sliding the final shell into the empty breech and praying I wouldn't need to use it. I retrained the rifle on the fallen figure, knowing it was too much to hope that the shot had killed it. There was no movement in the boat. Had I actually slain the fiend? Alas that it had to be at the cost of my shipmate.

I lowered the rifle and stepped back towards the wheel. Far off to the east the *Persephone* glowed like a false dawn. I watched as the mainstay collapsed, dragging the remaining mast with it. The falling masts appeared to stoke the fire within and I closed my eyes and imagined I might still feel some of the heat radiating from her. She had become a funeral pyre for the crew of the *Albin Grau*. It was a thought worthy of Dmitry.

I looked down to the boat and saw movement. In the dark I could see a pale hand clawing up and grabbing at the side of the boat. At first sight I felt a panic building within me, until I saw that it belonged to Dmitry. I looked over the rail and could see the Russian trying to pull himself upright.

"Dmitry!" I shouted. I took hold of the rope and started to pull the boat closer.

The Russian looked about him as if in a daze.

The oar left in the lock was now missing, either knocked from the boat by the waves or during the struggle. The remaining oar had snapped and only the shaft remained. He picked it up and, using it as a crutch, got to his feet. He was obviously injured, and I could see he was feeling very gingerly at the wounds inflicted on him by the creature. He looked at the pale thing still lying in the boat, brandishing the broken oar before him. He then turned to me and raised a bloodied hand as if trying to warn me of something.

"For the love of God, man; what are you doing?" I called out to him.

Before he could answer the creature behind him sat up. If he wasn't aware of it then the look of horror on my face must have alerted him. He dropped down onto one knee and wheeled about, holding the shaft of the oar defensively as one might a spear. I reached for the rifle leaning against the bulwark. The ship pitched over as I made a grab for it and sent the weapon clattering across the deck. I tried to reach after it but the rope in my other hand dragged me back.

I winced as the rough rope bit into my bare skin. I felt it tighten as I fought to hold the boat steady against the sudden surging wave. The line had looped around my hand and now held me fast. With my free hand I pulled at the rope, trying to stop it from stripping my flesh from the bone. It was pure luck that I had not been dragged overboard.

"Jump, Dmitry!" I shouted.

Through tears of pain and the spray of the squall I saw Dmitry look up at me.

"Please," I hissed through clenched teeth.

He regarded me, a strange serene look to his countenance that seemed at odds with the situation, and with the man in general. Behind him the figure raised itself up on its haunches and reached out to him. The Russian pulled a knife from his belt and, as the pale hands came about him once more, he severed the line between us.

My last sight of Dmitry was of him turning to face the monster – of him thrusting the jagged point of the broken oar deep into the naked breast of the thing as it fell on him. Then he was gone. The tiny boat was swallowed up by the boundless dark.

I remained there a long while, staring out over the crashing waves. My torn hand was bleeding so badly that the rope that hung from it had turned red. The buoy I had cast out still skipped over the schooner's milky wake like a flattened pebble. But there was no trace of the boat; it was a mere plaything for the petulant storm now. But then so was I. Wind-whipped brine stung at my eyes and elicited from them the tears that the misery at my desperate misfortune no longer could. I was numb. I had neither the strength nor the will to fight whatever fate placed before me.

I slumped onto the deck and bandaged my hand as best I could with a handkerchief. Above me, scornful winds howled and spat. I huddled on the quarterdeck, welcoming what meagre shelter it gave. Something metallic rattled across the planking. It was the rifle – it caught my foot as it slid by. Beyond the unmanned wheel I could see the bow rising and falling as the gale drew the ship headlong into the oncoming waves. I dragged the gun towards me with my heel until I could take hold of it. I embraced the weapon in both arms and felt the cold steel of the barrel against my cheek. One bullet remained. *Had fate engineered it thus?* I stared down into the muzzle.

~

I heard the mocking cries of gulls and opened my eyes to a painfully bright light. It was like staring directly into the sun. Then I saw the orb itself turn to black while the light radiating from it remained brilliant white. As my eyes adjusted I could see that the dark shape at the centre of my vision was the silhouette of a man standing over me. Behind him white sails rippled in a gentle breeze. Although I was struggling to focus, I was aware that he brandished a rifle and instinctively reached for my own. My hand grasped something on the deck, but it was not my gun.

"It's all right, you won't be needing this now," he said and I understood that the gun in his hands was my own. I made an effort to speak but could form no words, the chattering of my teeth reverberating within my skull, and the pain I had so mercifully been spared while unconscious started ebbing back into my limbs like a returning tide. The man, who still remained faceless to me, raised his voice and called to another behind him. "He's still alive, skipper."

"Well there go the salvage rights," was the reply and I heard several other voices raised in laughter.

Then a more serious sounding voice interrupted the merriment. "Skipper, you'd better have a look at this."

What happened next I am unable to recall with any certainty. As hands reached down to me and I was lifted to my feet, I felt the world about me start to spin and all sound, colour and light were sucked down as if into a maelstrom. I had succumbed to a fever, doubtless brought on by exposure and exhaustion. I spent the next few days lost in a delirium, the terrors I had escaped on the *Albin Grau* returning anew and continuing their dogged pursuit of my sanity. The faces of my dead crewmates loomed over me, pale hands reaching out to me from the darkest recesses, threatening to overwhelm and drag me back to that fate I'd so narrowly cheated.

At length the fever relinquished its grip on me and I awoke to find myself in unfamiliar surroundings. I lay not in a ship's bunk as I had expected, but a real bed. Through a gap in the linen curtains I could see the leaves fluttering in a light breeze, and beyond them a horizon that did not rise and fall to the whim of an ocean swell. It was only here during that long convalescence that I learned all the particulars of my rescue.

When the storm had finally blown itself out, I was many miles off-course and had strayed into the shipping lanes between the port of Kingston upon Hull and the Norwegian city of Kristiania. My salvation came in the form of the *S/S Avalon* of the Thomas Wilson line. It was not a proper ship to my mind, but a steamship, tasked with bringing in iron ore for the foundries of Sheffield.

I was taken on board in a delirious state and it was thought that I might not survive. The steamship towed the *Albin Grau* to the mouth of the River Humber. Here she was given over to the local authority to bring her into port, and it was from here the ship's owners were able to collect the vessel and her cargo, after a brief period under quarantine. I meanwhile, my fever finally broken, was placed under the care of the physician who had first attended to me on the steamship.

For a brief couple of days the events on the schooner became the talk of the town. Many lurid stories were proposed as to the fate of the crew. The more outlandish the tale the more it caught a hold of the public imagination, though none that I heard ever came close to the truth. There were one or two theories that I had some hand in their disappearance. Much later, when I finally got to hear the stories for myself, I wondered how much of this wild talk was taken as truth. On one occasion I had enquired of the doctor about the body of Nemetz, but he would not be drawn on the matter and changed the subject.

It was not yet the appropriate time, he told me, and would say no more about it.

Once I had recovered enough to walk some distance, it seemed that the appropriate time had arrived. I was requested to give my account of the events that befell the *Albin Grau* to the body appointed to investigate the disastrous voyage. I recounted the events as truthfully as I might, though I found that when I came to describe our unwelcome passenger, I told it as I had to the skipper after that first dreadful attack on Nemetz and didn't dwell on the more fantastical elements of my retelling. I imagine they would have had plenty of reports of my feverish ravings from my time on board the S/S *Avalon* and I felt no compulsion to injure my credibility further by regaling them with tales about monsters.

The outcome of the hearing was a forgone conclusion. The company's ship and cargo had been delivered intact, and to all present that was what really mattered. There were, of course, stirring eulogies to the bravery of the skipper and crew. It was agreed that I would still receive the wages owed to me – even though, as was pointed out, I'd delivered my ship to the wrong port.

The skipper's log had corroborated all that I had to say regarding the deaths of Nemetz and Gorski. It was the skipper's diligence in updating the logbook before setting out on that fateful mission which proved a godsend to me. As for what happened after that, it was my word alone, and I could see they had no reason or wish to question what I had said to them, though I could also see that some of those gathered before me expressed some dissatisfaction with my response to certain lines of questioning. I felt that I was there to do little more than tidy up an otherwise incomplete narrative and therefore draw a line under the whole tragedy. The conclusion drawn was that the crew of the *Albin Grau* had suffered attack from an unknown assailant on board the brigantine *Persephone*. And that in an attempt to apprehend the attacker, the *Persephone* was destroyed in a conflagration, wherein perished most of the crew. The assailant was described simply as a degenerate, possibly driven to madness by drinking seawater. When asked if I agreed with the conclusion I merely nodded.

I did garner some information about the mysterious brigantine we had encountered. The *Persephone* was, as I suspected, a Russian-registered vessel. It had departed the Romanian port of Constanța some three years earlier and had disappeared after passing through the Bosporus and into the Mediterranean. There had been a few unsubstantiated sightings in the intervening years, but the vessel had long been believed to be lost with all hands.

If I had expected to leave the meeting with a burden lifted from me then I was to be disappointed. I had, of course, been cleared of any culpability in the loss of the crew. But I knew my career as a seaman was over. It was not just the physical injuries I had received that determined this, though my mangled hand would regain none of the strength it once possessed, and I would forever bear the scar of that vicious rope like a vermilion serpent coiling about my wrist and palm.

The owners of the *Albin Grau* had expressed no objections to me remaining with the vessel. But even ignoring my own disability and the morbid revulsion I held at returning to a ship that had cost me so much, I was afraid to return. I do not deny it. But the decision for my future as a seaman would fall to any crew who would have me. And who of sound mind would now want to ship with me? I think the opinions of the trustees would change once they set to the task of finding a new crew for their vessel. Any sailor who survives when those around him have perished will always be looked upon with suspicion. I have yet to encounter any seafarer who will admit to a belief in good fortune – it is simply an absence of the bad.

I had become what the older sailors liked to call a 'Jonah'. A living embodiment of Coleridge's 'Ancient Mariner', my misfortune hung about me like that dead albatross. I imagine it would be an opinion that Dmitry himself would have held, and I would dishonour his memory to think it otherwise.

Secretly, it came as a relief to find that no ship would have me aboard her. I had no wish to return to the sea. Once I had revelled in the freedom of a constantly shifting horizon, now I felt only terror. I had lived all my life by the sea, and now even this proximity to it became too much too bear. With the constant roar of the breaking waves on the shore and the screams of the gulls overhead, even the sight of a distant ship upon the horizon would send my heart racing. Everywhere I turned there was something to assail my senses and stir up unfortunate memories. My nights spent alone became a demon-haunted realm, and I sought out what little solace I could find at the bottom of a bottle. When sleep did eventually find me, the room would roll and pitch about me as if I were sailing into the meanest of swells, and from out of the blackness, pale grey mottled hands would feel for me. I think it was a relief to my landlady when I left the lodgings I'd rented in Cromer and moved as far from the coast as I could manage.

~

And here you find me all these years later. No, I never returned to the sea – I haven't left this town in some fifteen years. But even here amidst this crowded beer house, if I shut my eyes for more than a brief moment, the memories return.

The sun is low to the west. I look out across an ocean that shimmers like quicksilver.

It is always with me. That is why I crave the company of people such as you. The more times I recount my story the less real it becomes to me. It has become a story to frighten children at bedtime, much like the tales my grandfather once told to me. Nobody believes the truth of it, and who could blame them?

I see a dark shape on the horizon.

No sir, even you... and there are times, particularly on such a fine day as we have just enjoyed, when I too think that the whole thing was some terrible dream that had manifested itself during my fever and which has scrubbed away the truth of the matter as if it were chalk upon slate. Have I spent the last twenty years of my life fleeing from a fiction or a crime?

Don't look so concerned, this isn't a confession. And if I had something as grave a matter as that to admit, I'd look to a more suitable establishment than this one. No, think no more of it. It was a story merely to entertain. The truth of it should not concern you. Or consider it a business transaction, if you prefer? A drink for me and, in return, you have a tale with which to send your children shivering to the comfort of their beds.

Here, you can take this to add some credence to the retelling. I was holding onto it when they carried me, half dead, from the deck of the *Albin Grau*. You don't smoke? Well neither do I. Think of it as a talisman or a good luck charm. It never worked for me of course, but a sailor believes only in bad luck or none at all. But I would hate to see it thrown away. It is a part of the story and I have passed that on to you now.

It's a ship that I see.

But I must be going – the light is beginning to fade and the night will soon be upon us and I don't like to be out after dark. Even after all these years, when the night draws in and the sounds and bustle of the daytime have subsided, my thoughts still return me to the *Albin Grau*. Eventually I shall slide into sleep, the footfalls of the other lodgers on the floors above and going up and down the stairs all mingling to become the creaking timbers of the ship. I feel the room turn about me as my failing balance invokes in me the illusion of the sea's motion.

There are two pale hands, one steadily being placed over the other, climbing up the swaying rope from out of the darkness.

And it is then that I shall see its approach and shall awaken, calling out that same name night after night. For it is not the creature that comes to me, though those seemingly disembodied hands might well be his. No, for as the apparition comes closer I see that they are but a part of a mechanism that is advancing along the rope. All the while the head is turned away from me, concentrating on the labouring tangle of arms and legs. Having disengaged itself from the rope, it then crawls up over the end of the bed.

And I look into the dead, unblinking eyes of the Russian.

I now know why Dmitry sacrificed himself; I know how it was that the crew of the *Avalon* discovered poor Nemetz. Not as I had last seen him, oh no, but emergent from the shredded remains of his makeshift shroud like some befouled Lazarus. His pale twisted limbs thrusting outwards as if reaching towards something or someone. The hollow face with its mouth gaping wider than nature could allow. And with a sharpened belaying pin transfixing the sailor's chest.

Neil Williams was born in Cheshire and still lives there with his wife and daughter.

Lightning Source UK Ltd.
Milton Keynes UK
UKHW011931280421
382793UK00001B/31